Collect all the PiPER REED books

Book One

Book Two
(formerly *Piper Reed, the Great Gypsy*)

Book Three
(formerly *Piper Reed Gets a Job*)

Book Four

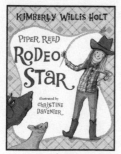

Book Five

Book Six

KIMBERLY WILLIS HOLT

Piper Reed
Forever
Friend

Illustrated by
CHRISTINE DAVENIER

Christy Ottaviano Books
HENRY HOLT AND COMPANY
NEW YORK

Henry Holt and Company, LLC

Publishers since 1866

175 Fifth Avenue

New York, New York 10010

mackids.com

Henry Holt® is a registered trademark of Henry Holt and Company, LLC.

Library of Congress Cataloging-in-Publication Data

Holt, Kimberly Willis.

Piper Reed, forever friend / by Kimberly Willis Holt ; illustrated by Christine Davenier. — 1st ed.

p.   cm.

"Christy Ottaviano Books."

ISBN 978-0-8050-9008-6 (hc)

[1. Moving, Household—Fiction. 2. Family life—Virginia—Fiction. 3. Friendship—Fiction.

4. United States. Navy—Fiction. 5. Norfolk (Va.)—Fiction.] I. Davenier, Christine, ill. II. Title.

PZ7.H74023Pif 2012   [Fic]—dc23   2011033500

First Edition—2012

Printed in the United States of America by R. R. Donnelley & Sons Company, Harrisonburg, Virginia

1 3 5 7 9 10 8 6 4 2

To Shannon, my first reader
(who happens to be the best daughter),
and to Jerry, forever and ever

—K. W. H.

CONTENTS

1

A Fish Tale

In December, Chief got his new orders from the U.S. Navy. We were moving to Norfolk, Virginia. I'd be saying good-bye to the Gypsy Club that I started here, but since Michael and his twin sister, Nicole, had moved to Norfolk last month, I already had two friends there. Enough for a new Gypsy Club. I couldn't wait for my new adventure to begin.

When we moved to Pensacola, Florida, fifteen months ago, there'd been five of us—

Chief, Mom, my sisters Tori and Sam, and me. Now two more had joined our family—our dog, Bruna, and Sam's goldfish, Peaches the Second.

Bruna would be moving with us, but not Peaches the Second. Sam pitched a big fit when Chief broke the news. "That's not fair! Just because Peaches the Second is a fish?"

"Sam, just think about it," I said. "This is what it would be like for Peaches the Second trapped in a plastic bag on a long car ride." I sucked in my cheeks and crossed my eyes. Then I rocked side to side.

Even Tori glanced
up from her poetry
book and laughed.
And she hardly ever
cracked up at any-
thing I did. I guess
thirteen-year-olds
don't have a sense of humor. At least I
had three years to go before I lost mine.

Chief patted the spot next to him on the
couch. "Come here, Sam."

Sam plopped near him, but crossed her arms
over her chest. "But, Daddy, what's going to
happen to Peaches the Second?"

I placed my hands over my heart,
trying to look sad like someone at a
funeral. "Most goldfish eventually
experience the great flush in the
sky," I said.

"The what?" Sam asked.

My fingers flushed an imaginary commode handle in the air, and I said, *"Ker-plunk!"*

Sam burst into tears.

Tori slammed her book shut. "Piper Reed, you are mean!"

"Piper," Chief said, "you aren't helping matters." He wrapped his arm around Sam and said, "Sweetheart, the drive would be too long for Peaches."

"Peaches the Second," Sam corrected him.

Chief hit his forehead with a flat palm. "Of

course, Peaches the Second." Then he winked at me. "Yes, she could . . . uh . . ."

I began to sing the only funeral song I could remember. "In the sweet by and by . . ."

Chief lowered his eyebrows at me just as Mom walked into the room with a laundry basket.

"Why don't you give Peaches the Second to Brady?" I asked.

"That's a great idea, Piper," Mom said. "Brady loves Peaches."

"THE SECOND!" Sam yelled.

Mom sighed. She was sorting through the laundry, tossing the unmatched socks into a pile. Chief kept a sack of unmatched socks and tried to match them up each time he did laundry. He called it the Single Sock Looking for Love Sack. Mom ignored the sack and threw them into her art bag for sock puppets or some other art class project.

When Tori had found out, she'd said, "Mom's and Dad's sock systems totally contradict each other."

"Yep," I'd said, "and that's why the Reed family goes around sockless most of the time."

Then Mom pitched one of my favorite socks in her art project pile, the one with jets all over it.

"Wait!" I dashed across the room and rescued it. Once the sock was safe in my hands, I asked Sam, "So what do you think about giving her to Brady?"

"But I don't want to give Peaches the Second to him," Sam whined. "Then I won't have a fish." She puckered up her lips and started that pretend cry she used whenever she couldn't get the tears to come.

Chief stood up and headed toward the kitchen. "Sam, if you give your fish to Brady, we'll buy you a new one when we get to Norfolk."

Sam wiped her phony tears with her shirttail. "How about two?"

The pantry door squeaked open, and Chief pulled out a loaf of bread. "Okay, two goldfish."

Sam should be a lawyer. She knew how to get Chief to cave in. He was at his weakest when he was hungry.

"Everyone grab a plate," Chief called out. "I'm making tuna fish salad sandwiches for dinner tonight."

"What?" Sam squealed. "How could you?"

"Chief didn't say goldfish sandwiches." A picture of Peaches the Second flopping between two pieces of rye bread flashed in my mind, and I started laughing.

"What's so funny?" Sam asked.

"Nothing," I said. "It's kind of a private joke."

Tori chuckled. "That sounds fishy."

Even I cracked up. That was the first time in her entire life my big sister, Tori Reed, said anything funny.

2

Last Day

Moving to Norfolk would be like no other move. Usually when Chief was assigned to a different place, I had to make all new friends. The best part about these orders was that Michael and Nicole were already there. Maybe they had started recruiting members to the Gypsy Club. Then it would be the biggest and best Gypsy Club in the world. My heart skipped beats just thinking about that.

Thursday was my last day at the Blue Angels

Elementary School. We couldn't have a going-away party at school because most of the students were military kids. If we had a party every time someone moved, we'd be throwing a party every couple of weeks. Although in my opinion that would be a lot more fun than learning about history and fractions. My last day kind of felt like a party anyway because everyone was super nice to me. Even mean ole Kirby, who was never nice.

At recess, Stanley said, "I can give you my e-mail address again if you lost it. All of my friends in Norfolk must have lost mine when I moved here. I haven't heard a word from them."

"I still have your e-mail address, Stanley. You and Hailey will be the first ones that I write. Of course it might take me a while since I'll be unpacking, and I'll have to visit Michael and Nicole. We'll have a lot to catch up on."

Stanley's shoulders lifted. "Don't forget my

grandfather lives in Virginia Beach, which happens to be very close to Norfolk."

How could I forget? Stanley had been telling us ever since Michael and Nicole learned they were moving there.

At the end of the school day, Ms. Gordon said, "Piper Reed, good luck in Norfolk. We'll miss you." When she said that, her eye didn't twitch one bit.

I didn't want Ms. Gordon to be sad. So even though she wasn't my favorite teacher, I said, "If you give me your e-mail address, I'll write to you."

Ms. Gordon stared at me a long second. Then she opened her desk drawer and she wrote her e-mail address on a tiny Post-it note.

I could hardly read her itsy-bitsy scribble. So I had to spell it out loud. "Does this say *d-i-s-c-o-l-i-v-e-s* at wired dot com?"

Ms. Gordon nodded, and this time I noticed

her left eye twitching. She really ought to see a doctor about that. She might have some terrible eyeball affliction.

Earlier that day, my reading teacher, Ms. Mitchell (who was my favorite teacher), gave me her e-mail address and a book of short stories about dogs, the only kind of stories I think are worth reading. I would miss Ms. Mitchell, and when she said good-bye, she held out her hand and said, "Piper, it has been a pleasure to work with you. You're one of the smartest people I know."

"I am?" I really was surprised when she said that. Tori made straight A's, and Sam was practically a prodigy. But no one had ever said I was one of the smartest people they knew.

"Yes, Piper, you're very smart. Never forget that."

"Am I one of the smartest kids in the school?"

"Yes," she said.

"In Pensacola?"

Ms. Mitchell smiled. "No doubt."

I couldn't stop myself. I needed to get a handle on this smart thing. "How about Florida?"

She laughed. "Oh, Piper Reed, I'm going to miss you."

After school, Hailey and Stanley came over to my house to say good-bye. It would also be my last Gypsy Club meeting in Pensacola.

"Let's say the Gypsy Club Creed," I told them. "I want to make sure you get all the words right so that after I leave, you can still have club meetings."

"I know all the words," Hailey said.

Stanley, the newest member, scratched his head. "I think I do, but maybe we should say them just in case."

Hailey sighed real big, like she would rather be anywhere else but my bedroom reciting the creed.

I looked at her, waiting.

"Okay!" she said.

We stood, saluted, and began:

We are the Gypsies of land and sea.
We move from port to port.

We make friends everywhere we go.
And everywhere we go, we let people know
That we're the Gypsies of land and sea.

After we finished, Stanley said, "Maybe my family will move to Norfolk again."

"That would be awesome," I said.

"Ours won't." Hailey blew a big bubble, popped it with her finger, and chewed. "My dad's tour of duty ends in June. Then we're moving back to Wisconsin near my grandparents. I'll get to be with them every day."

"Lucky." My grandparents lived in Louisiana. We wouldn't get to see them again until they visited us in the summer.

"Maybe I'll get to see you at spring break," said Stanley. "We might go to my grandparents' in Virginia Beach. Until then I'll e-mail you."

"Great," I said, even though I knew that meant I'd be receiving an e-mail from Stanley every single day.

"I'll e-mail you, too," said Hailey. "Well, I better say good-bye. I have a lot of homework." She stepped forward and hugged me.

Before we parted, Stanley yelled, "Group hug!" Then he joined in, wrapping his arms around us, pressing his cheek against the back of my head.

Hailey and I shook loose, causing poor Stanley to stand there hugging the air.

"Come on, Stanley," Hailey said. "Piper probably needs to pack."

I watched them step away, and that silly lump I had in my throat when Michael and Nicole left for Norfolk came back. I hated good-byes. My life had been filled with them. If your dad or mom is in the Navy, saying good-bye is part of your life.

When Stanley's and Hailey's sneakers met the sidewalk, they swung around and faced me. Then they cupped their hands around their mouths and yelled, "One, two, three—GET OFF THE BUS, PIPER REED!"

That night, our next door neighbors Yolanda and Abe invited us over for a good-bye dinner. Brady showed Sam the spot where he planned to keep Peaches the Second's bowl. He pointed to a place on a table in front of the living room window.

"Peaches Two can look outside," he said.

Sam's hands flew to her hips. "Her name is Peaches the Second."

"Peaches Two is her nickname," said Brady.

Uh-oh. Too bad Brady didn't wait until Sam left to give that goldfish a nickname. Then he could have called her Rocky or Scarface or anything he wanted. But Brady was three, and he hadn't caught on to Sam's controlling ways.

Sam looked from the spot on the table to the window. "*Peaches the Second* will get too hot in front of the window. She'll fry."

"Is that what you call a *fish fry*?" I asked.

Yolanda giggled, and Abe shook his head, grinning. "Oh, mercy!" he said. "Piper, we're going to miss you."

"Yes, we are," Yolanda said.

Gosh, it seemed everyone in Pensacola was going to miss me.

3

MILE MARKERS

Friday we left NAS Pensacola for NS Norfolk. Before we got in the car, Mom handed Abe our camera and asked him to take a picture of us all in front of our home.

"This makes number nine for Karl and me," Mom said. She wiped a tear from her left eye as she gave Yolanda another quick hug.

It was my sixth move and Tori's eighth. I studied our front yard, where my sisters and I had ran through the sprinkler system the day

Chief left for ship duty over a year ago. That was just one of the memories I'd made here. Mom said our lives were like quilts. Each patch represented a place we'd called home, and each stitch was a memory that would always bind us there.

"We'll stay in touch," Yolanda said.

Dad shook hands with Abe, and my sisters and I gave Brady a big squeeze. He promised Sam he'd find a good spot for Peaches the Second. Then he ran over to Bruna and pointed his finger at her and said, "Woll over!"

And of course, Bruna did. She always listened to Brady.

Before we pulled out of the driveway, I said, "Don't forget to set the trip odometer, Chief."

"Thanks, Piper."

Chief set it to zero, then he started the engine.

"And don't forget to say good-bye to the street," Sam said.

Without saying a word, Chief made a last round on our street and tapped the horn about a dozen times. It was our tradition. We did it every time we moved. Abe, Yolanda, and Brady waved at us from their front yard.

"I'll miss Brady," said Sam. "I'm glad I gave him Peaches the Second."

Just as we turned the corner, I saw Hailey and Stanley parked on their bikes. They waved their arms high, and Hailey honked the horn on her handlebars. *Trring, trring, trring.*

I waved back, and Chief sounded the horn one more time.

"I'll miss my friends," I said. "And the Blue Angels."

"I'll miss my students," Mom said.

"Who will you miss most, Tori?" I asked.

She didn't answer me, so I turned around to look at her. I was going to say, "Will anyone miss you?" But just as I opened my mouth, I stopped. She was staring down at her book, but I could tell she was crying. Probably over some boy. Probably over Stanley's brother Simon, who could do no wrong. Still, seeing my big sister with tears dropping on her book made my gut hurt. I turned and faced forward.

Chief glanced in the rearview mirror. "I'll miss McDonald's," he said.

Then we all laughed, even Tori, because, of course, no matter where we were, there was always a McDonald's.

As we drove past the front gate, I saluted the guard, even though he didn't see me. "I'll be back," I whispered, "when I'm a Blue Angel."

Mile 41

Bruna finally calmed down and curled up on the floorboard. For the first forty miles, she'd stared out the back window and barked at every passing car. She always did that, as if every car might be smuggling a cat.

Sam plugged her fingers into her ears. "Peaches the Second would never do this."

"Peaches the Second is a goldfish," I said. "Goldfish don't bark."

"I hope Brady remembers to feed her," Sam said.

I sighed. "I hope Brady remembers

not to *overfeed* her like someone I know once did to a poor helpless goldfish."

Sam glared at me. Then she opened her book, *On the Banks of Plum Creek*, and began to read.

I turned toward Tori, waiting for her to snap at me, but her earbuds were stuffed inside her

ears, and her head was bobbing to the music on her MP3 player. This was going to be a very long ride.

Mile 427

While Tori ignored the whole family, Sam insisted on reading every sign we passed. Thanks to her, I knew how far it was to every gas station and fast food restaurant. Even though my sisters drove me crazy, the thing I liked best about traveling with them was each night we squished together in a hotel bed like olives packed in a jar. Sometimes Tori told one of her stupid stories, which put me to sleep quicker than counting sheep. Her stories were so boring, I could hit dreamland in three minutes flat.

And the thing I liked next to the best about staying in hotels was waffles with strawberries and whipped cream. That was like having dessert for breakfast and a whole lot yummier than Mom's homemade healthy granola with flaxseeds.

Before we got back on the road the second morning, Tori and I went to the hotel's business office to check our e-mail. I was hoping to find one from Michael. He'd e-mailed me only once since I told him we were moving to Norfolk.

When we headed toward the office, Chief called out, "Make it fast, girls. We need to be on the road by o-eight hundred."

Tori took forever reading her e-mail from all her poetry club friends. I tapped my foot.

"Okay, okay," she said. "Just one second, and I'll be finished."

Finally it was my turn. I had only one e-mail. It was from Stanley. And it was surprisingly short.

Dear Piper,

    I miss you and Bruna. Pensacola hasn't been the same since you left. Hailey doesn't want to be in the Gypsy Club anymore, and a club isn't a club unless there is more than one person.

        Your Gypsy Club pal forever,
        Stanley

P.S. Tell Sam I went over to Brady's and
checked on Peaches the Second. She (or is
Peaches the Second a guy fish?) is still
alive and swimming.

I was disappointed I didn't receive an e-mail from Michael, but now I was more down about there not being a Gypsy Club in Pensacola. I'd worked hard to start that club. I made invitations and recruited members like a good leader. How could Hailey drop out? Something had to be done. Stanley had to find more members, members that would be true to the Gypsy Club Creed.

When I got back to the van, I decided this wouldn't happen in Norfolk, Virginia. First of all, our club already had three members— Michael, Nicole, and me. Our mission would be to make this Gypsy Club the biggest and best ever. Knowing Michael, they probably already had twenty members. I couldn't wait to find out. I hoped Michael, Nicole, and I would be in the same class like fourth grade at the Blue Angels Elementary School. Even if we weren't, I'd get to see them every lunch and recess.

At NAS Pensacola, the officer housing, where they lived, was only a few streets away from the enlisted housing where we lived. I hoped it was that way in Norfolk.

I decided to write a list.

Things I Hope Happen in Norfolk, Virginia

1. I hope Michael and Nicole are in my class.
2. I hope Michael has started the Norfolk branch of the Gypsy Club.
3. I hope there are at least twenty people in the Gypsy Club.
4. I hope we can walk to the beach like we could in Pensacola.
5. I hope I have my own room.
6. I hope Tori's MP3 player earbuds get stuck inside her ears.

4

~~~

A Good Sign

Mom and Chief wouldn't tell us a thing about our new home. They wanted everything to be a surprise. Maybe the enlisted housing was mixed with the officer housing and Michael and Nicole would be our next-door neighbors. At mile 859, we drove past a sign that read NORFOLK, VIRGINIA.

Finally Tori pulled out her earbuds. Oh, well. I didn't expect everything on my list to come true.

Chief drove by the base. "We'll tour the base tomorrow."

"We aren't living on-base?" I asked.

"No," Chief said. "The military housing is located off-base."

Two and a half miles later, we drove into a neighborhood with white townhomes attached together. They looked like a row of sparkly clean teeth.

"Your new neighborhood, Gypsy girls," Mom said.

Chief slowed the van to a worm's pace as Mom read the addresses. "Twenty-seven eighteen, twenty-seven twenty, twenty-seven twenty-two . . . here it is."

The homes were bigger than the ones at NAS Pensacola. Maybe I wouldn't have to share a room.

Then it was as if Sam read my mind, because she asked Mom and Chief, "Can I have my own room?"

"I guess you'll have to count the bedrooms," Mom said and smiled at Chief.

Did that smile mean what I thought it meant? All three of us dashed out of the van and headed toward the front door. A guy who looked about Tori's age sat in a lawn chair in the yard next door. He was strumming a guitar, and his face hid behind his long hair. Tori slowed her pace like she couldn't care less if she had her own room. She glanced over at him, but when he looked her way, she quickly stared at the ground.

I knew an opportunity when I saw it. "First one inside gets her own bedroom," I hollered.

Tori's focus snapped back toward the house, and she broke into a wobbly-legged sprint. Sam was close behind me, but I touched the doorknob first. Of course it was locked. Mom and Chief walked toward us. Chief dangled the keys in the air. "Forget something?"

"Beat you," I told Tori when she finally caught up.

Tori's face was red from the dash. She didn't like to break a sweat. "It doesn't matter that I came in last. I'm the oldest, and I'll get my own room."

Chief slipped the key in the keyhole. "What if there are only two bedrooms?"

"You mean all three of us might have to share a room?" I asked. Sharing with Sam was bad enough, but how would I survive messy Tori,

who dropped her clothes and
everything else on the floor?
I'd have to dodge her shoes like
I was walking through a
land mine.

The van
windows were
down, and
Bruna poked
her head
out and barked.
Then she turned
to face the other
end of the street, and barked
like she was letting every dog in the neighborhood know she'd arrived. It worked. Soon we
could hear a whole chorus of barks from the
surrounding yards.

"Piper, go get Bruna," Mom said. "She's
probably ready to do her business."

Figures. My one shot at my own bedroom, and I had to walk the dog.

I snapped Bruna's leash on and lifted her out of the van. The second I put her down on the grass, she started to do her business—on my shoe. I quickly moved my leg to the side and shook my foot. "Hey, don't get mad at me. I tried to get us our own room."

"Make way, girls," Chief said. "We aren't going to break a Reed family tradition."

"Oh, Karl!" Mom said, blushing.

Chief lifted Mom into his arms. She locked her hands behind his neck. He carried Mom into the house and

set her down a few steps into the foyer. No wonder Tori was so mushy over boys. Mom and Chief acted like they were Romeo and Juliet.

We went from room to room—the family room, the kitchen, the dining area, the bathrooms, the laundry room. Sam climbed the stairs ahead of me and soon yelled, "Here's one big bedroom!"

"Ours," Mom and Chief said. Their words bounced against the walls of the empty rooms.

Sam rushed to the next room. "Bedroom number two!"

"Mine!" Tori hollered. She hadn't even bothered to go upstairs. Must be nice to be the oldest.

"Bedroom number three!" Sam continued.

I groaned as I caught up with her. I studied the empty room and imagined a line down the middle. "Mine and yours."

"Nope," Sam said. "This one is *mine*."

"And just where do you think I'm going to sleep?"

Sam pointed across the hall to another room. "There!"

I rushed through the doorway. The room was a little smaller than Sam's, but the window looked out over our backyard, which I thought was a fair trade-off. I floated around the room and whispered, "My very own room."

Getting my own room was the first thing to come true on my list! This was a good sign.

5

MEETING THE NEIGHBORS

Mom was unpacking the box of groceries we'd brought from Pensacola. "Where do Michael and Nicole live?" I asked her.

"They live at Lake Estates. It's a short drive from here."

"Drive?" I gulped. "They don't live in our neighborhood?"

"This is enlisted housing, Piper. Most of the officers' families live in civilian housing in Norfolk."

I was proud that my dad was a chief petty officer, but I wished we could live in civilian housing, too. Why couldn't we live in Michael and Nicole's neighborhood?

"Cheer up, Piper," Mom said. "They'll still be a part of your life. We're going to see Michael and Nicole tomorrow. The Austins invited us over for lunch."

It wouldn't be the same, though. I couldn't walk over to their house, and they couldn't walk over to mine. The first thing that didn't happen on my *Things I Hope Happen in Norfolk, Virginia,* list.

In the backyard, Bruna made her way around the entire area, sniffing the grass next to the fence line. Then she turned around and sniffed her entire way back. When she discovered a hole in one of the pickets, she stuck her nose through it for a whiff. Just as quick as she did, Bruna yelped and backed away from the fence.

I ran over, bent down, and peeked through the peephole. A big, fat white cat stared back. He stuck his paw through for a swipe, but I pulled away in time. Bruna had better watch out. That cat looked like it had eaten a few dogs in its lifetime.

Bruna barked at the hole, but she didn't stick her nose through it again.

"You might want to stay clear of cats that are bigger than you, Bruna."

She inched a bit closer to the hole and growled.

Bruna would have to learn to accept that the cat was probably there to stay. Just like I'd have to learn to accept that Michael and Nicole were not going to be my neighbors in Norfolk. At least we'd have school. Maybe one of them would be in my class. We could have Gypsy Club meetings at recess and lunch. Maybe it wouldn't be that different.

Upstairs, I noticed Tori peeking between her window blinds. Seemed she was as nosy as Bruna about what was going on next door. She didn't even hear me when I walked over and peered over her shoulder. I should have known. She was goggling at the boy next door, who was in his backyard strumming a guitar.

"He's not that cute," I said. "Unless you like the hairy-legged mop-head type."

Tori gasped, then swirled around. Her face was red. "Get out of my room!"

I took a giant step back from my crazy sister, whose hands had rolled into fists. Sometimes I thought my sister was training to be a boxer. If she kept eating so much, she could become the Heavyweight Champion of the World.

Tori charged toward me. "I said get out of my room!"

I've never run so fast backward. As soon as I reached the hall, the door slammed in my face.

"Guess that's what you call a Peeping Tori," I said through the door.

"You are forbidden from my room forever!" she yelled from the other side.

I tapped lightly on the door just because I knew it would irritate her. I was right.

Tori kicked the door three times.

We were at war, and the door was the enemy boundary line.

I tapped softer.

She kicked four times.

"Hey! Cut that out!" It was Chief coming up the stairs. "We've got neighbors to consider. We share walls, and they don't want to hear your fighting."

I wondered about the neighbors. I wondered if any kids my age lived next door or just Tori's new crush and a slap-happy cat.

The moving van showed up a couple of hours later. I settled on the curb and watched them unload our stuff. A little girl with strawberry blond hair in braids strolled over. Two purple bandages formed an *X* across each knee.

"Do you have any sisters or brothers?" she asked.

"Two girls claim to be related to me. One is a grumpy boy-crazy teenager. The other is a spoiled brat who likes goldfish."

"How old is the spoiled brat one who likes fish?" she asked.

"Six," I said.

"I'm six, too," she said, rocking on her feet. "Is she a lot spoiled or just a little bit?"

"Oh, I guess you'll find out sooner or later." I walked to the house, opened the front door, and hollered, "Sam! There's a girl out here who wants to meet you!"

Sam rushed out of the house. "Where is she?"

A moment later, the two of them sat on the grass together. Sam named everything that the

movers carried into the house. "That's my bed. That's our sofa. See that purple spot? Piper spilled grape juice on it when she was eight years old."

"For goodness' sakes, Sam. She doesn't want to know about every piece of furniture that's going into our house."

"Yes, I do," said the little girl. "Whose lamp is that?"

Sam smirked at me. Then she quickly turned toward her new friend. "Tori's. She's my nice sister." Then she asked, "Do you like goldfish?"

I don't know why I felt so grumpy about Sam having a new friend. Maybe it was because I'd moved all this way believing two of my best friends would be living in my neighborhood. Since I wouldn't get my driver's license for at least six years, I'd have to depend on Mom or Dad to take me there.

A tall girl with bright red hair walked up to Sam's new friend. "Hey, pipsqueak! Time to get your heinie home for dinner."

The older girl looked my way. "Hey," she said. "Welcome to the neighborhood."

"Thanks," I told her.

"I'm Arizona," she said, holding out her hand.

I wasn't used to kids doing that, but I took hold of it and shook hard.

Arizona looked impressed. "You've got quite a grip on you."

"Thanks," I said. "Are you named after the state?"

"No, silly. The ship. My great-grandfather was serving on it the day Pearl Harbor was attacked."

"Get off the bus!"

Arizona wrinkled up her nose and glanced around. "Huh? What bus?"

"Oh, it's just something I say when I'm excited."

Arizona shrugged. "That's bizarre."

My face burned. Suddenly, for the first time ever, I felt kind of goofy saying *get off the bus*.

Arizona turned and focused on her little sister. "Zinnia, get over here on the double."

"Was Zinnia named after a ship?" I asked.

"No, silly. The flower. Gosh you're a funny kid." She sounded like she was so grown up.

"How old are you?" I asked.

Arizona frowned. "Hey, didn't anyone tell you it isn't nice to ask someone their age?"

"Well . . ." My cheeks felt hot all over again. Living in Norfolk was a lot different than living in Pensacola.

Then her face broke into a grin. "I'm just joking. I'm eleven."

That meant she was probably in sixth grade and would be in middle school with Tori. I thought about calling up to Tori to tell her she had a new friend, but instead I asked, "Do you want to be an official member of the Gypsy Club?"

"The Gypsy Club? What's that?"

"It's a club for kids whose parents are in the military. We're Gypsies because we move all the time."

For a second, I
imagined Arizona
jumping up and
down and yell-
ing, "Yippee!
Really? Me? You
want me to be in
your club? That
would be great!"
I thought she'd
be happy like
Stanley was when
he became a member.

He'd even memorized the Gypsy Club Creed
before he was officially asked to join.

Instead Arizona's eyebrows shot up. "A
club?" She said *club* like it was the dumbest
thing she'd ever heard.

I studied the ground, digging my toe into the
grass. "Well, we really do fun things together."

"I'll think about it," Arizona said. Then she looked in the direction of Sam and Zinnia. "Come on, squirt!"

Zinnia finally came over to Arizona, and the two of them walked away. Suddenly Arizona turned around and asked me, "Hey, what's your name anyhow?"

"Piper. Piper Reed."

She looked up at the clouds for a second, then said, "Well, see you later, Snapper."

"It's Piper," I said, but it came out so quiet that Arizona didn't hear. Watching her walk off, I wasn't so sure I wanted to see her later. Anyone who didn't get excited about being invited to join the Gypsy Club could probably never be a good friend of mine.

6

~~~

NEW THiNGS

Saturday morning I woke up early. We were going to Michael and Nicole's house. I slipped out of bed and peeked through the blinds. It was still dark outside. The streetlight glowed against the rooftops. I was probably the only person in the entire neighborhood who was awake. Then I noticed the neighbors' cat creeping out from under a bush.

The clock on my bedside table read 3:29.

I ran toward my bed and pounced on top of

the mattress, then jumped four times. If I wasn't going to be a Blue Angels pilot, I could probably win a gold medal in gymnastics at the Olympics.

Bruna leaped off the foot of my bed and looked up at me with sleepy eyes. When she realized I wasn't going to let her outside, she curled up on the floor and went back to sleep.

I glanced at the clock again—3:31. The rest of the family would be asleep for a while, but I decided to go ahead and get dressed. I opened a drawer and pulled out a clean shirt and jeans.

Michael and Nicole loved the Gypsy Club as much as me. Arizona was going to miss out on all kinds of fun. Now that I was in Norfolk, we could have our first official meeting tomorrow.

I pulled up the blinds. Then I sat on the edge of my bed and waited for the sun to rise. A yawn slipped from my mouth. *Maybe*, I thought, *if I just stretch out on my bed for a li . . . ttle . . . while. . . .*

Before I knew it, I heard Mom calling, "Piper, wake up! It's ten o'clock. You need to get ready."

"What?" I rubbed my eyes and slowly opened them.

Mom was standing in the doorway. "Don't you remember? We're going to Michael and Nicole's house today."

I threw back the covers and jumped out of bed.

"Ready, ma'am." I saluted her.

My mom's mouth dropped open. Then she asked, "You're already dressed? Did you sleep in those clothes?"

"I changed earlier. I just took a little catnap." In five minutes, I gobbled down Chief's pancakes, brushed my teeth, and rushed downstairs.

Of course, as usual, we had to wait for Tori. When Tori got ready, she acted like she was going to meet a movie star. I could just imagine what was going on behind that closed door. She was probably combing her hair a hundred strokes and brushing her teeth, flossing, and gargling. (Every dentist we've had has loved cavity-free Tori.) The only makeup she was allowed to wear was lip gloss, and she took *forever* to put it on. I guess it takes years of practice to make sure the shiny stuff doesn't slide off your lips. I tapped my foot and sighed.

Sam ran up and down the stairs.

"Come on, girls," Mom hollered.

Finally, Chief yelled to the top of the stairs, "Victoria Reed, get down here on the double."

Tori came downstairs. Yep, sure enough, her lips were shiny.

"Everyone in the van," Chief said.

I crawled in the back and buckled my seat belt.

Tori's perfume took up all the fresh air.

I pinched my nose. "Yuk! I can't breathe. What's that stinky smell?"

Tori frowned and said, "Happy."

"Well, it doesn't make me happy," I said.

Sam leaned toward our big sister and took a long whiff. "I think Tori smells good."

"Thank you," Tori said, then she turned around and glared at me. "Some people clearly have better taste than other people."

"That's for sure," I said, fanning my face.

"Can I wear some Happy, too?" Sam asked.

"Sunday maybe you can wear a little to church," Tori told her.

"You're the best big sister in the whole wide world," Sam said.

Fine by me. I didn't want the Best Big Sister in the Whole Wide World Award anyway.

As I watched from the window, I felt like a bunch of bubbles were filling up inside me, that floaty feeling you get when something exciting is about to happen. After a while, some of that feeling started to fade. I looked at the odometer. We'd driven seven miles. Mom was wrong. It wasn't a short drive to the Austins' neighborhood.

Finally Mom said, "Here's the street."

We turned into a neighborhood with colorful bungalows and sprawling yards. Some of the houses were on the bay.

"I'll bet they can have German shepherds here," I said. Before we got Bruna, I'd wanted a German shepherd. But our yard and house had been too small, so we got a poodle instead. Not that Bruna wasn't special. She'd kind of grown on me.

We came up to a green house with burgundy shutters.

"Here it is," Chief said.

Before we parked the car, Nicole rushed out of the house. Her parents followed, but Michael was nowhere in sight.

I beat Tori out of the van. "Hey, Nicole."

Nicole gave me a hug. After we finished with the hellos and hugs, Mrs. Austin said, "Come on, everyone. Let's go inside for hot apple cider. We'll have lunch in an hour. Hope you like pot roast." Sometimes I forgot that Mrs. Austin was a lieutenant commander. I probably should have saluted her, but she just seemed like a regular mom to me, someone who made apple cider and pot roast.

Nicole grinned real big. "Don't you notice something different?"

I studied her for a long moment, my gaze going from head to toe. Something about Nicole did look different, but I couldn't figure out what the different part was.

"Did you get a new haircut?"

Nicole shook her head. "You're close, though." She smiled again, flashing her white teeth. She must brush her teeth as much as Tori.

Then I knew. Each of Nicole's teeth was perfectly straight. "What happened to your braces?"

"It was time for them to come off."

"Get off the bus, Nicole!" I raised my palm, and she slapped it.

"I miss picking out the rubber bands, though." Nicole used to choose different colors for the holidays. There had been black and orange for Halloween, pink for Valentine's Day, red and green for Christmas, and purple just because it was her favorite color.

I glanced around the house, searching for Michael. Maybe he was hiding. Maybe he was about to bounce out from behind a sofa and yell, "Surprise!"

When our parents and my sisters gathered into

the kitchen for a cup of hot apple cider, I finally asked Nicole, "Where's Michael?"

"He's skateboarding with Douglas. He's supposed to be back soon. Let's go to my room."

"Who's Douglas?"

"He's Michael's new friend. He lives down the street. They skateboard together every day."

Like a needle, Nicole's words popped every bubble of excitement I felt when we first started toward their house. My best friend was too busy with his new friend to welcome me. Maybe Norfolk wasn't going to be fun, after all.

As if she'd read my mind, Nicole said, "You'll love living in Norfolk. It's a fun city. They have a great zoo, and downtown they have boat rides."

She sounded like they'd lived in Norfolk for years, but her family had only moved there a month ago. I guess it was long enough for Michael to have forgotten about me and all the fun we'd had in the Gypsy Club.

All of a sudden, I heard a familiar voice calling out, "Piper! Piper Reed!" It was Michael.

He walked into Nicole's room, wearing a red helmet and a skateboard. "Hey, Piper Reed! Welcome to Norfolk, Virginia." He smiled at me, and all those bubbles returned in one big swoosh. He wore a blue windbreaker with a skateboard logo. Then he stepped aside, and I saw another boy holding a skateboard and wearing a red helmet. His windbreaker was an exact copy of Michael's. Nicole and Michael were twins, but it looked like Michael and his new friend wanted to be.

"This is Douglas," Michael said.

"Hey," Douglas said, raising his hand.

"Hey," I said, so softly I didn't even recognize my own voice. I felt like I was shrinking.

"What do you think of Norfolk?" Michael asked.

I shrugged.

Michael lightly punched my arm. "Gosh, when did you get so quiet?"

"We just moved here." Now the words croaked out like a frog. What was happening to my voice? What was happening to me?

"I was just telling her how much fun it is to live here," Nicole said.

Maybe *here*, I thought. Here, living in a house near the bay and having a new friend who is teaching you to skateboard.

Then I don't know what made me say it, but I couldn't help myself. Maybe I was just longing for the way everything used to be when Michael, Nicole, Hailey, Stanley, and I were standing in our meeting place near the flagpole at the Blue Angels Elementary School. Maybe I was thinking about what Stanley said about Hailey not wanting to be in the club anymore. All I know was I had to say it. So I blurted out, "Let's make today our first official Gypsy Club meeting in Norfolk."

Douglas wrinkled his nose. "Gypsy what?"

Michael laughed nervously. "We can talk about that later." He turned toward Douglas and asked him, "Do you want to stay for lunch?"

"Sure, it smells great." Douglas squatted and pushed his skateboard, causing it to roll across the room and slide past Nicole's dust ruffle. It stopped somewhere under her bed. Then Michael shoved his in the same direction.

"I guess we can talk about the club at school Monday," I said.

"School? Are you going to St. John's, too?" Douglas asked.

"St. John's?"

"We're going to St. John's," Nicole said. "I told you in my e-mail."

My mouth hung open, but no words came out. I guess I'd thought it would be the same school as mine. The rest of the afternoon I didn't say anything, not when we ate lunch in the Austins' solarium, not when I watched Douglas and Michael skateboard up and down their street. And when Michael asked if I wanted a turn, I just shook my head.

"Come on," Douglas said. "We'll show you how to do a manual. After you learn that, we'll show you the half pipe at the park."

"It's awesome fun," Michael said.

But all I could think about was how I missed all the old fun.

7

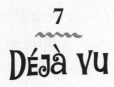

DÉJÀ VU

Back at our new home, Mom and Chief talked about volunteering at the Norfolk Botanical Garden. "I was looking online at the information, girls. Tori, you and Piper could help, if you wish."

Tori looked as if Mom had said she would have to plow fields. Her eyes popped wide. "I'll think about it. But I'm sure I'll have a lot of homework this year."

"What about me?" Sam asked. "I want to volunteer."

"I'm afraid you're a bit too young," Chief said. "You'll have to wait until you're ten."

"I have a volunteer job for you," I said.

"What?" Sam got so excited she dropped her fork on the floor.

"You could straighten Tori's messy room. It already looks like a tornado hit it."

"Very funny," Tori said. Then she folded her arms across her chest. "Wait a minute. How do you know?"

"Hey," I said, "what do you expect? We just moved here. I accidentally thought it was my room." While my big sister let out a long, dramatic sigh, I tried to imagine volunteering at the botanical gardens. What could be fun about that? Maybe I'd volunteer to keep Tori's room clean instead.

Tomorrow would be our first day of school.

Mom was going with us, so that after registering us, she could apply for substitute teaching work. Between visiting the Austins and dinner, Chief had taken Sam to the pet store, where she bought two goldfish. Sam named them Romeo and Juliet. That night Sam sat at the kitchen table with paper, crayons, and scissors.

"What are you doing?" I asked her.

"Making invitations," she said, not even bothering to look up.

"We just moved here, and you're already planning a party?"

"I'm making invitations for a club."

Sam was doing exactly what I had done in Pensacola, the night before my first day of school, the exact thing that I had hoped to do here in Norfolk. After today, I didn't feel like it.

"What club?" I asked her.

"*My* club. The Goldfish Club."

I read over her shoulder.

Do you own a goldfish? If the answer is yes, you're invited to join the Goldfish Club. Contact Samantha Reed for details about our first meeting.

"Samantha? So now you're Samantha, not Sam?"

She looked up, frowning. "My name has always been Samantha."

"Okay, Sa-man-tha. Just how many people do you think own a goldfish?"

"Probably millions."

I shook my head and walked away. "Well, Sam, I guess tomorrow you'll find out."

"SAMANTHA!" she corrected me.

I thought about the time I made invitations for the Gypsy Club. That next day I'd met Hailey, Nicole, and Michael. Now Michael didn't seem to want to be a Gypsy Club member. He had his new friend, Douglas, and his skateboard. Plus now that he and Nicole wouldn't be at my school, we couldn't have meetings at recess.

The next morning I awoke with a funny feeling. Maybe I had a sore throat. I swallowed. It was kind of sore. Sort of. Maybe I had a stomachache. I thought about being the new kid at school all over again. My stomach did kind of ache. Maybe I had a fever. I felt my forehead. It did feel kind of hot. It was official. I was sure I had some terrible disease. I wouldn't be able to go to school.

Unless I was practically dying, Mom would never let me stay home from school. I jumped out of bed and raced around the room. I ran so fast beads of sweat dripped down my cheeks. Now my face felt hot. Hot as a fever. I stretched out my arms and twirled. My room became a blur. I felt dizzy. My stomach began to spin. I fell back on the bed just as Mom opened my bedroom door.

"Piper, why aren't you getting dressed?"

"Ohhhh," I groaned. "My head feels hot, and my stomach is wheezy." That wasn't a lie. Then I added, "I'm probably too contagious to go to school today."

Mom came over to my bedside and sat on the edge. "You are red in the face." She touched my cheeks with her cool fingers. "You're burning up."

"And don't forget about my stomach."

"That's a shame. Your dad made pancakes
for breakfast."

"Yeah," I said, then I groaned. "Pancakes
don't even sound good this morning." I lied. I
loved Chief's pancakes. They were the best
pancakes in the whole world.

"You better stay home today. After I take
Sam and Tori to their schools, I'll call a doctor."

"A doctor? You don't need to do that. I bet

it's one of those twenty-four-hour diseases. You'd hate to infect all those other sick kids in the waiting room when I'm going to be as good as new tomorrow morning."

Mom stared at me a long moment, her eyebrows knitted together. She gently brushed my hair away from my face. "Hmm. I bet I know what you have. And I think you might be right. It probably will only last twenty-four hours. But if you aren't better by this afternoon, I'm making an appointment at the base clinic." She stood to leave.

"Thanks, Mom," I said with a raspy voice. "I'm sure I'll be better this afternoon."

"Do you have a sore throat, too?"

"No, ma'am," I said, returning to my regular voice. No use in overdoing it.

She looked at me a long moment and headed toward the door. "I'll be back in about an hour, but I'll put the cordless phone by your bed. Call me if you need anything."

Chief had already left for work, and when I heard Mom leave with my sisters, I rushed downstairs to check out the leftover pancakes. The dishes and frying pan were piled in the sink. The counter was wiped clean, but there wasn't a pancake in sight, not even a crumb. Gosh, you get sick, and your sisters gobble up your pancakes. Now my stomach really did hurt. I was hungry. I glanced into the pantry and found the potato chip canister. After grabbing a handful, I went back upstairs to bed. I wished I had a television in my room.

About an hour later, Mom came home with a folder. "I met your teacher. Ms. Hamburger is really nice. I'm sure you'll like her. I told her you were sick and asked if she could give me your assignments so you wouldn't fall behind."

This day was not starting out so great. No pancakes, no television. Just lots of homework from a teacher named after fast food.

"She gave me your textbooks, too. I'll get them out of the car. Do you feel like eating?"

"I'm kind of hungry," I said.

"I'll heat up some chicken soup."

"Thanks, Mom."

A list formed in my head.

Why You Shouldn't Pretend to Be Sick

1. *You miss out on the world's best pancakes.*
2. *You still get homework.*
3. *You get canned chicken noodle soup.*
4. *You have to go to school the next day anyway.*

At least I got to do my homework in bed. Mom even placed a large bed tray across my lap for a desk. The first thing I learned right off—one fluffy pillow plus one soft mattress plus a bunch of boring homework equals one sure fine nap.

"Pssst . . . hey, Snapper."

I opened my eyes.

Arizona stood in the doorway. Was I still dreaming?

"Hey, Snapper, how come you didn't go to school today?"

No, I wasn't dreaming. Arizona was still calling me by the wrong name.

I sat up so quickly, all my papers and the math book fell to the floor. "Um . . . I was sick," I told her.

She walked into my room and picked up the book. "If you'd come to school today, you'd be done with this stuff already. Our teacher did half the assignment with us."

"*Our* teacher? Don't you go to the middle school with Tori?"

"Middle school?" Arizona stood. "Nah, I'm in your fifth-grade class. I'm just tall for my age. Really it's just my legs. The rest of me is pretty much fifth-grade size."

I stared at Arizona from head to toe. She was right. She was practically all legs. And a lot of kids turned eleven in fifth grade.

"Yeah," she said, "I'll bet I know what you had," she said.

I waited.

"Newkiditis."

"Newkiditis?" It sounded contagious and deadly.

"Newkiditis is the dread of being the new kid. Most Navy brats catch it at least once or twice. I've never had it, though."

The hairs on the back of my neck began to prickle. Who did she think she was, a doctor? I knew everything there was about being a new kid. I moved all the time. I was an expert at being a new kid.

"Yep," she said. "Looks like you have a bad case."

"Well, I've never had that," I said. "For your information, I had the seven-hour flu."

"Oh?" Arizona started to back out of the room. "You sure?"

"Yes, but you might want to leave now, in case I sneeze on you." I wiggled my nose. "In fact, I feel a sneeze coming on right now."

"Well, I don't want to get sick. I've got my bowling league Tuesday night and my stamp-collecting swap meet on Friday." Arizona turned to leave. "See you later!"

"Alligator," I added softly as her footsteps pounded downstairs.

When I heard the front door shut, I jumped out of bed. Maybe there would never be a Gypsy Club in Norfolk, but I'd show Arizona that I was an expert new kid. I'd join the bowling league, even though the last time I bowled I got a total score of seventeen. And although I had no idea what a stamp swap meet was, I'd go there, too.

Mom walked by my room, then stopped and stuck her head in. "You're up? Are you feeling well?"

"I've had a miraculous recovery," I said. It was true. That visit from Arizona had worked better than any medicine. Now I was on a mission—a mission to be the champion of new kids.

8

GYPSY CLUB, ANYONE?

Arizona Welch was the tallest girl in our class. She was taller than my new teacher, Ms. Hamburger, who didn't look anything like her name. I would think anyone with the last name Hamburger would be round and have pickle green hair and mustard yellow skin. Instead Ms. Hamburger had pretty brown hair and wore sparkly eye shadow and raspberry-colored lip gloss.

Even though Arizona was taller than Ms.

Hamburger, she didn't slouch over like she was ashamed of it. She stood up straight like she couldn't wait to be tall enough to poke her head through the ceiling and gaze at the birds. I guess that's why she thought she was an expert on everything, including newkiditis.

Ms. Hamburger didn't make a big deal about presenting me in front of the class like Ms. Gordon had in Pensacola. Instead she just said, "Welcome, Piper. We're glad to have you."

Then she told the class, "Most of you have a parent or

both parents serving in the military, so you know what it's like to be new. Please make Piper feel at home."

Every kid in the class stared back at me. I could picture each one of them saluting and reciting the Gypsy Club Creed. I wished I'd made invitations to the Gypsy Club. I was missing a great opportunity.

Ms. Hamburger told me that I could sit at the empty desk at the back of the class, which is the very best place to sit. At the back you could see everyone in class, like a captain overlooking his crew on a ship. Arizona sat at the back too, probably because no one could see over her head. If she sat up front, she'd block the blackboard or the flag or Ms. Hamburger when she was talking about something interesting like the Jamestown colony field trip we'd be taking next month.

When the bell rang for lunch, Arizona asked

me, "Want to go with me to the book club? I'm sure the librarian won't mind."

"That's okay. I don't care much for reading."

"Really?" Arizona acted like I'd said I hated chocolate-chip cookies (my favorite food in the whole world) or riding roller coasters (which would be one of my favorite things in the world if I'd ever ridden one).

"Sure you don't want to join? It's an interesting book."

"Is it about a dog?" I asked.

"Nope," she said.

"No thanks," I said, before she could tell me what the book was about. "I only read dog books."

Arizona laughed. "Snapper, you sure are funny." She walked down the hall, tapping her brown paper sack lunch against her leg while I headed in the opposite direction to the cafeteria.

"See you at bowling tonight!" I hollered after her.

She turned around. "What did you say?"

"Bowling. I joined the bowling league. Hope my team doesn't smear yours. I was the star player in Pensacola." Just then my mind pictured Mom's pink bowling ball rolling down the gutter. Again and again.

"Razzle-dazzle! Then I'll see you later," Arizona said and started to walk down the hall again.

"Alligator!" I hollered, but there was so much noise from the kids rushing to the cafeteria, I don't think she heard.

I imagined Arizona was thinking about how she hoped my team didn't beat hers. But I really didn't have a regular team. I wasn't even a regular member. Mom had called the base bowling center last night and gotten in touch with the bowling league coach, who said I could be an alternate player. Someone was always sick or missing, so she thought I'd get to play every week.

Then I told Mom I wanted to go to the stamp swap meet that met at the recreation center. She got excited. "Oh, I've kept a box of Uncle Leo's letters from all over the world. You can have the stamps from the envelopes."

I had no idea what those stamps could be swapped for, but I was hoping something cool like tickets to the amuse- ment park, where I could finally ride a roller coaster.

9

GUTTER BALL CHAMP

After school I did everything in slow motion. I was hoping that if I did everything slow enough, I could stop time and not have to go bowling. How could something that sounded like such a get-off-the-bus idea yesterday seem like such a dumb idea now? The number seventeen flashed in my mind. How could I help my team win with gutter balls? How could I beat Arizona, who probably got all strikes and spares?

I inched home, so pokey that Sam said,

"Hurry up!" Then I brushed my teeth, tooth by tooth. It took so long that Tori pounded on the door. "Are you alive in there? Other people need to use the bathroom."

Tori was moving as fast as I was slow. When I opened the door, she barged in and slammed the door behind her. A few seconds later, she was out and dashing down the stairs.

"I'm leaving, Mom!" she hollered.

"Good luck!" Mom called back.

I wondered what exciting thing Tori had going on. When a person has something fun to do, they move quick, and when they're doing something not so fun, they move slow. Bowling should be fun. If only I hadn't bragged that I was a star player in Pensacola. If only I knew how to bowl a strike. Maybe I could practice. But it was an hour before dinner, and I had to leave right after we ate. What would a Blue Angel do who had to practice a flight formation and couldn't get to the airfield? Then suddenly I knew.

Visualization! Visualization was kind of like imagination. Visualization could make things happen. I stretched out on my bed and closed my eyes. I saw the pink bowling ball in my hands. I saw myself running down the lane and stopping right before the dark line. I saw the dark arrows pointing toward the pins. I saw me picking out the middle one and letting go of the ball. I saw the ball rolling over the middle arrow and heading toward the pins. I saw the ball hit the center pin. I saw the first pin fall, then the second, the third, fourth, fifth, sixth, seventh, eighth, ninth, tenth. I saw myself jump in the air and holler, "Strike!" I saw my team stand up and cheer my name. I saw Arizona's team cry.

Over and over, I visualized my strike. I didn't even look at the clock, and before long,

Mom was hollering, "Piper! Your turn to set the table for dinner!"

Sam was at the kitchen table with her pile of invitations. She had marked through *Do You Own a Goldfish?* and replaced it with *Do You Love Goldfish?* Now she was crossing through *Love* and replacing it with *Like.*

"What's the matter?" I asked, "You didn't find a million goldfish owners at our school?"

Sam glared up at me. "Where are all *your* new friends?"

I hate it when a six-year-old has me pegged.

I folded my arms across my chest. "You need to get your stuff off the table if I'm going to set it for dinner."

Sam cleared away her invitations, and I put the cloth napkins, bowls, and silverware in their spots. "Where's Tori?" I asked Mom.

"At the zoo. She's trying to get a volunteer job as a junior docent."

The last time we went to the zoo, Tori complained about having a headache because of "all the stinky animals."

"What does a junior docent do?"

"I don't know," Mom said. "I guess we'll find out."

Just as Mom placed the bowl of carrot soup

on the table, Tori burst into the house and yelled, "I got it! I got it! I'm a junior docent."

"Congratulations!" Mom said.

"That's my girl," Chief said.

"Will I get to go to the zoo for free?" asked Sam.

"No, but you can come see me work. I'm in charge of the elephant cart."

"That figures," I said. "Make sure to leave some peanuts for the elephants. No one likes a skinny elephant."

Tori ignored me, but as she joined us at the table, she said, "The elephant cart educates the public about elephants. It also talks about how Asian elephants are endangered because of poachers." She sounded like she was reciting the junior docent handbook. Then Tori added, "Sam, if you want, you can have your birthday party at the zoo. I can help with that, too."

"Hey," I told her, "I should be a junior

docent. I'm the one with party-planning experience."

"You're not old enough," Tori said smugly. "You have to be thirteen." I'll bet she couldn't wait to tell me that.

Mom scooped some of the thick soup into my bowl. "That was nice of Tommy to tell you about the job."

"Who's Tommy?" I asked.

"The guy next door," Tori said as if I had forgotten the name of the president of the United States.

"Oh, now I get it," I said.

"What?" Tori asked. "You get what?"

"Nothing," I said. Then I took a big slurp of soup. Now I knew why Tori was so interested in volunteering at the zoo. She wasn't excited because of the elephants or the birthday parties. Her excitement had everything to do with a boy named Tommy.

After dinner, Chief drove me to the base bowling alley. "I think it's great how you're already jumping in and joining things. That's what it takes to make new friends when you move to a new place. But I guess I don't have to tell you that. You're an expert."

At least I didn't have to convince Chief I knew how to be a new kid. Now all I had to do was convince Arizona.

Chief walked me in and met the sponsor before driving home.

Mrs. Lehman was a tiny woman with a big voice that boomed over the loud country music and the falling bowling pins. "Hello, Piper. We're so glad to have you join our league. Next season I'll have a regular spot for you on a team, but today I'm going to have you play with the Nighthawks."

I smiled and followed her over to a team of girls and boys wearing black T-shirts with NIGHTHAWKS in red letters across the front.

"Nighthawks, Piper is filling in for Lenny tonight. Arizona, could you please show Piper the ropes?"

I gasped, almost choking on the big gulp of air.

"Sure thing, Mrs. Lehman."

When Mrs. Lehman walked away, Arizona said, "Hey, Snapper, looks like we won't have to lose to you after all."

I was speechless. This wasn't what I had

planned at all. There were six teams in the league, and I had to end up on the one with Arizona.

Arizona was first to bowl. She must have done this a zillion times, because she took hold of her ball with three fingers as easily as someone picks up a cantaloupe at the grocery store. She positioned the ball under her chin and squinted her eyes. Then off she glided toward the boundary line and let go. The ball kited down the lane, staying straight on center, until it hit all ten pins. *Clatter, clatter, crash!*

"Strike!" she yelled, then turned around to her teammates, who stood and clapped. "Way to start us off, Arizona," said one girl. This was my visualization, only Arizona had invaded it.

I stood, too. Not because I was applauding her, but because it was my turn next. Or, rather, it was Lenny's turn. That was the name on the electronic scoreboard.

After I picked up the ball, I tried to remember everything I'd seen in my visualization, but instead I saw myself racing past the boundary line. I saw myself racing past the boundary line and throwing the ball before I noticed the center arrow. I saw the ball heading toward the arrow on the far left and not stopping until it hit the gutter. I saw it rolling all the way until it fell out of my sight. And that's exactly what happened. I sure hoped Lenny was the kind of guy who got a lot of gutter balls.

"Aw, Snapper. That's a tough break. Don't worry, I'm sure you'll pull it together next time."

But when the ball returned to me, I did the same thing. Each turn my mind replayed my

messing up, and each turn I bowled gutter balls.

Here's how the only two players' scores that mattered to me looked:

Arizona: 10 9 10 7 10 8 10 8 10
Lenny: 0 0 0 0 0 0 0 0 0

On Arizona's last round, I closed my eyes. It took a second, and I had to squeeze my eyelids together real tight, but finally I made the gutter lanes disappear. They didn't exist. Then I saw myself pick up the pink bowling ball; glide to the boundary line, concentrating on the center arrow; release the ball; and watch it roll down the lane until it hit the center pin and all the rest.

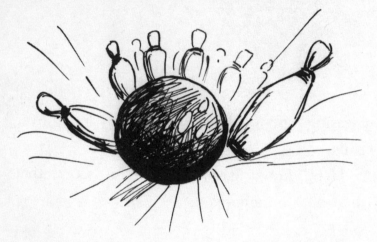

"Hey, Snapper, are you asleep?" Arizona asked.

I opened my eyes.

"It's your turn, Lenny," said one guy. "Gee, I wonder what your score will be?"

But I didn't pay any attention to him. I focused on my visualization and went over to get my ball. I whispered the words. *Pick up, glide, release, strike.* And that's exactly what happened. *Clatter, clatter, crash!* I froze, right there at the boundary lane, looking at my beautiful strike. My strike. Lenny's strike. A strike that had started in my mind before I ever picked up the ball. This visualization thing was real powerful stuff.

I turned around, and every Nighthawk was clapping for me. "Way to go, Snapper!" Arizona said.

I almost forgave Arizona right then and there. Almost forgave her for saying I had newkiditis and for calling me Snapper, but then she added, "You were probably just nervous since you were the new kid."

Just wait, I thought, just wait until I make a better swap than you at the stamp swap meet tomorrow night.

10

STAMP SWAP MEET

Friday night, I went downstairs to wait for dinner. Mom dropped pasta in a pot of boiling water, which meant it was Italian night.

Sam stood on the chair, shaking flakes into the fishbowl. Romeo and Juliet swam toward the surface, catching the food as it dropped. Meanwhile Bruna sat staring at the spot on the floor next to Sam, probably waiting for some flakes to drop. Bruna was better than a vacuum cleaner.

Sam jumped down from the chair. "Mom, can I make gold cupcakes and lemonade for my club?"

"Sure," Mom said. "But how about orange cupcakes? That's almost gold."

"Okay," Sam said. "Goldfish are kind of orange."

"How many people do you think you're going to have for the first meeting?" I asked Sam.

"Twelve."

"Twelve? You think twelve people want to be in a club about goldfish?"

"I gave out twelve invitations."

"That doesn't mean you will have twelve people at the meeting," I told her. "Did they say they would be here?"

"Well, they didn't say they wouldn't."

"I guess you'll find out tomorrow. Don't get your hopes up, though." When I said those words, I felt mean.

"You're just jealous because I have a club and I'm going to make lemonade and orange cup-cakes."

Maybe Sam was right. Maybe I was jealous.

The sun had already set when it was time to go to the stamp swap meet. So Mom walked with me to the recreation center. I held Uncle Leo's envelopes in a box with a rubber band securing the lid. The entire way there, Mom talked about all the places Uncle Leo had sent those letters from.

"He never said much of anything that made sense to me in those letters, but it was exciting to receive mail from South America and Africa. Promise me when you grow up and go somewhere interesting and do amazing things, you will always send me some letters."

"You got it, Mom." Even my mom knew I was capable of interesting and amazing things. And now I knew how it could happen—visualization. I'd already visualized swapping Uncle Leo's stamps for amusement park tickets so I could ride a roller coaster.

When we got to the recreation center, Mom said, "Your dad will pick you up in an hour. Have fun. I think it's neat that you want to collect stamps."

Collect stamps? Mom must have thought I was a terrible swapper if all I would come home with would be a bunch of old stamps.

Arizona was there and about a dozen other people. A few were adults. "Hey, Snapper, you didn't tell me you were a stamp collector, too."

"Actually that's what I'm here to unload."

Arizona lifted her eyebrows. "What do you mean?"

"Stamps. I'm here to swap some stamps."

"Exactly," Arizona said. "That's the spirit."

An old man who wore his glasses at the tip of his nose said, "What do you have, young lady? The new kids always bring the best merchandise."

I opened the box, revealing Uncle Leo's stamps.

"South America!" The old man was clearly impressed. "Now we're talking."

"Razzle-dazzle!" said Arizona. "And they're still on the envelopes."

"And Africa, too," I said. This was probably going to be a better swap than I'd even hoped for. But I hadn't forgotten how a swap worked. "What do you have to offer?" I asked the old man.

The old man opened his box and pulled out five plastic sacks. "They're mostly domestic, but this sack has European ones."

I stared down at the stamps.

"I'd like a chance to trade, too," Arizona said. She showed me some stamps with Amelia

Earhart and some with Navy subjects. I had to admit they were amazing, but not as great as amusement park tickets.

Now the other people had crowded in, trying to get my attention. But the only thing they had to swap were stamps.

"Doesn't anyone have anything else besides stamps to swap?" I asked.

Every head that had been staring at my stamps lifted up and looked at me.

Arizona started to laugh. "Snapper, this is a stamp swap. Don't you want stamps?"

"No," I said. "I'd like something else, like maybe . . . amusement park tickets."

Arizona and the old man stayed, but the other people shrugged, turned, and walked away.

The old man put his hand in his pocket for his wallet. Then he opened it and pulled out twenty dollars. He held it out to me.

"Sir," I said, "if you make that thirty, you have a deal."

He hesitated, but then added a ten.

Arizona laughed again and shook her head.

Half an hour later, Chief arrived, and I left with my money. Arizona might be laughing, but she couldn't deny that for a new kid, I was a pretty good swapper. I would be riding a roller coaster in no time at all.

11

GOLDFISH CLUB

Saturday morning I went downstairs and turned on the computer. I hadn't checked my e-mail in a whole week. There were three messages waiting—one from Hailey and two from Stanley.

Hailey bragged about how they were going on a cool field trip. I wrote back and told her we were going on a field trip, too.

Then I read Stanley's first e-mail.

Dear Piper,

*I miss you and Bruna. Please give her
a Liver Lump and tell her it's from me.
Because you know if I were there or if you
were here, I'd give her a Liver Lump. Or
two. Or three. I keep trying to have a
Gypsy Club meeting, but no one wants
to be in the club.*

On and on he went, telling me about his
perfect brother, Simon, who had won another
trophy, this time for a literature contest where
he received first place for a short story.

Then Stanley told me all his homework
assignments. Reading about homework assignments is almost as bad as having to do them.

The last e-mail from Stanley was short.

Dear Piper,

Are you getting my e-mail?

I didn't feel like answering Stanley. I didn't know what to say to him to cheer him up. I missed the Gypsy Club, too.

I walked into the kitchen where Sam was sitting at the island, drinking a glass of chocolate milk and writing down things in a notebook.

"What are you doing up so early?" I asked.

"Getting ready for my club."

I straddled the stool next to her just as the doorbell rang.

"Oh, my goodness!" Sam hopped off her stool and set her milk glass in the sink. "I didn't think anyone would be here this early. I haven't put out the napkins yet."

The doorbell rang again.

"Aren't you going to answer the door?" I asked her.

She dashed frantically around the kitchen. First she went toward the container of cupcakes. Then she opened the refrigerator and stuck her head in. She closed it and then looked down at her pajamas. "How can I answer the door? I'm the hostess. I have to get ready."

Mom and Chief were still upstairs. I left the kitchen and answered the front door, expecting to find a mom and a six-year-old. Instead I discovered a little kid standing alone. He must have ridden his bike over, because I could see a small green one on our lawn.

"Hi." I held the door open with an outstretched arm, and the boy walked underneath my arm, heading toward the living room.

"Uh . . . can I help you?" I asked.

He plopped on our couch. "I'm here to go fishing."

"Fishing?"

"The fishing club." He leaned over and picked up the remote control, which was on the coffee table, and flicked on the television.

"I think you have the wrong club," I said.

He changed the channels until he found a cartoon with a blue rabbit skipping.

Finally I closed the door and settled down on the couch next to the boy. "What's your name?" I asked him.

"Stevie Sherman."

"Do your mom and dad know you're here?"

"They're working on a ship."

"Who do you live with?"

"My grandma," he said, not even looking up. His eyes were glued to the television.

"Does your grandma know where you are?"

"She's asleep."

Sam had changed and was now setting the table, putting down the pink place mats.

"Sam," I said, "you have a guest."

Sam straightened the place mat and folded a napkin on the side. "I don't know him."

"His name is Stevie Sherman. You gave him an invitation."

"No, I didn't."

"Well, he's here, and he thinks that this is a fishing club."

Sam stopped folding the napkins. Her face turned red, and she yelled, "THIS IS NOT A FISH- ING CLUB. THIS IS A GOLDFISH CLUB. YOU HAVE TO LIKE GOLDFISH!"

Even with Sam yelling, Stevie Sherman didn't hear her. He was too busy laughing at the television screen.

Tori came downstairs dressed in jeans, a T-shirt, and Converse sneakers. This was the ear- liest I'd ever seen her up on a Saturday. She must have had a huge crush on Tommy to get up early to talk about elephants. When she reached the bottom step, she asked, "What's all the racket?"

Stevie Sherman looked up at Tori. "Hi! Are you Samantha?"

Sam yelled from the table, "I'M SAMAN-THA!"

"You're beautiful," Stevie Sherman told Tori.

Tori blinked three times. "I am?"

"I think you might be the most beautiful girl in the whole world," Stevie told her.

"Well, thank you," Tori said, and despite the fact that she spent half her life staring in the mirror, she really seemed surprised.

I was surprised, too. I didn't think of Tori as beautiful. I didn't think of her as ugly either. To me, she was just grumpy boy-crazy Tori.

"I'm Stevie Sherman," he said. "I'm five years old."

"It's nice to meet you, Stevie Sherman. I'm

Tori Reed." She headed toward the front door, then turned around. "You sure are a nice little boy."

When Tori left Sam said, "You're five?" She didn't sound happy about that. "Five-year-olds are not invited to this club."

I glared at her. "Can I see you in the kitchen, Sam?"

She didn't come until I said, "Samantha?"

In the kitchen, I leaned against the dishwasher. "Sam, whether you like it or not, Stevie Sherman is here, and you're going to have to let him into your club."

"You didn't let me into your club because you said I was too young. He's five years old, and that's too young for *my* club."

"You're six. What is one year going to hurt?"

"Kindergartners don't know as much as first-graders."

Just then Mom walked in. "What is that little boy doing here so early?"

"Why don't you let Mom decide if Stevie Sherman should be in your club?"

"What?" Mom asked, muffling a yawn. She filled the coffeepot with water.

Sam knew I had her trapped.

"Okay. You win," Sam said. "Stevie Sherman

can be in my club today. But I'm not promising that he can be in it forever."

I wanted to tell her no club was forever. It seemed the Gypsy Club was never to be again.

An hour later, eleven six-year-olds showed up with their moms or dads. Even Pipsqueak Zinnia came. Bruna wagged her tail as each one arrived. She must have thought they were here to see her.

When Mom found out that Stevie hadn't told his grandmother where he was, she asked for his phone number so she could call his grandma.

"I don't think I can give you that," he said.

"You don't know your phone number?" Mom asked.

"I know it, but I'm not allowed to give it out to strangers."

Stevie Sherman must have forgotten the part where you don't walk into strangers' homes and turn on their television without asking.

Mom handed the phone to Stevie. "Why don't you dial your number, and I won't look. Then you can hand the phone to me so I can speak to your grandmother."

Stevie thought about that for a while. "I guess that will be okay. You're not a kidnapper or anything like that, are you?"

"No, I'm a mom."

"Are you Tori's mom?"

Mom nodded, smiling. "Yes, and Sam and Piper's."

Stevie dialed the number, glancing up often to make sure Mom didn't peek. Then he handed the receiver to Mom.

After she hung up, Mom said, "His grand-mother was wondering where he'd wandered off to. She said he does it all the time."

I could tell Sam loved being in charge of twelve kids, but I thought I'd better hang around just in case she needed my help. After

all, I was an expert on clubs. I'd started two of my own.

I plopped down outside their circle, pretending to look at a magazine.

Sam said, "Now that it's time to start, I should call roll."

"Is this like school?" one boy wanted to know.

"A little. We need to call roll and make up rules."

"I don't like school," the boy said.

"Me neither," said Zinnia. "If this is going to be like school, I don't want to join."

"Well, it's not exactly like school," Sam said.

"I think I want to go home," said a girl.

The kids stood to leave, all the kids except for Stevie Sherman, who clearly didn't have anywhere else to be.

"I need to call my mom so she can pick me up," Zinnia said.

Like a chorus round, the rest of the group said, "Me too."

Panic spread across Sam's face. Then she looked at me with a look that said *I need help, but I'm never ever in a million years going to ask for it.*

Right then and there, I decided that no matter how snotty Sam was and no matter how many mean things she'd said to me or how many mean things I'd said to her, she was still my little sister.

I opened my mouth and said the words that were as strong as a secret weapon. "Who wants orange cupcakes and lemonade?"

Then twelve little kids stopped heading to the front door and rushed to the dining room table instead. In mere seconds, they sat waiting for me to serve them a cupcake.

And even though Samantha, who used to be

Sam, didn't say thank you, I plopped a cupcake in front of her and said, "You're welcome very much."

Sam had a lot to learn about clubs. She may have started the Goldfish Club, but it was not just her club. It belonged to all the members. And she needed to be open to new ideas and things. She'd find out, sooner or later. I left Sam's club and settled in front of the computer.

I opened my e-mail and started my letter to Stanley.

Dear Stanley,
  I miss you, too. So does Bruna. I promise
to give her some Liver Lumps and tell her
they are from her pal, Stanley.

Then I told him about how I had my own room, how I'd seen Michael and Nicole and

met a girl named Arizona. I closed by telling
Stanley what I had also wanted to say to Sam.

*You just need to be open to new ideas and
things.*

And that's when it came to me. I needed to
take my own advice.

New Things to Try in Norfolk
1. *Go bowling for fun, not just to impress
   someone with my great bowling skills.*
2. *Try stamp collecting (after all, there are
   Amelia Earhart and Navy stamps, too).*
3. *Try skateboarding.*

12

You Can Be a Volunteer Too, Piper!

Dinner that night might as well have been named the Tori Reed Supper because it was all about Tori. All through the meal, Mom and Chief asked her about her day at the zoo.

I would have been sensational as a junior docent. I had birthday-party-planning experience. I watched the Animal Planet channel. I knew all about elephants, monkeys, and tigers. I didn't blame animal smells for headaches.

Of course Tori's room was as messy as a baboon's cage, so maybe she was meant to work at the zoo.

Tori talked about the elephant cart and Tommy, Tommy, Tommy, Tommy, Tommy, Tommy.

"I'm proud of how you are giving back, Tori," Chief said.

"Thank you," said Tori, who had hardly eaten a bite of her dinner.

"In fact," Mom said, "you've reminded us of our decision to volunteer at the botanical garden. We're going to go next Saturday, and, Piper, we'd love for you to join us."

Of course the only place I was old enough to volunteer would be a garden.

"Do they have any animals there?" I asked.

"I'm afraid not," Chief said. "Or at least I don't think so."

"Oh. Not even birds?"

"Well, they may have birds," Mom said. "We'll have to see."

"Excuse me," Sam said. "Just where am I going to be if everyone is volunteering? You can't leave me home all by myself."

Mom smiled. "Sam, I've talked to Stevie Sherman's grandmother. She said you could stay with them. You'll get to spend the day with Stevie."

"Stevie Sherman is five years old," Sam said. "Couldn't I stay with the Welches?"

"Actually, Mrs. Sherman is babysitting—I mean Zinnia is staying there, too," Mom said. "The Welches have other plans on Saturday."

"What kind of things do volunteers do at the botanical garden?" I asked.

"Weeding and mulching are two things," Chief said.

"Weeding and what?"

"Mulching. That's when you add mulch—a material that keeps a lot of the weeds from growing around the plants."

Weed stopping didn't sound fun at all. "I could babysit Sam."

Sam smacked her fork against the table. "Hey, I'm not a baby."

"Piper, why don't you come with us at least once? If you don't want to go again, you won't have to."

At bedtime, I added to my list.

> 4. *Go mulching with my family. (Every*
>   *new thing you try can't always be fun.)*

13

A-Mulching We Will Go

The next Saturday, Tori went off to the zoo, Sam went to Stevie Sherman's house, and the rest of us went to the Botanical Gardens.

I started to sing a song I'd made up. "A-mulching we will go, a-mulching we will go. Hi-ho, worm-a-phobe, a-mulching we will go."

Mom joined in the second round, but Chief said, "I don't think I know that song."

Singing that song together made me think

mulching might not be so bad after all. Then we turned on the winding road that led to the gardens. We parked the van by some other cars.

"Look," Mom said. "We aren't the only family that came to mulch today."

We hopped out, and Chief crawled in the back to get our wheelbarrow.

"Do you need help with that, Mr. Reed?"

It was a familiar voice. My heart began to race, and when I walked to the other side, I discovered I was right. The voice belonged to Michael. Douglas was standing next to him. My heart sank a little.

"Hi, Piper," Douglas said. "Did you come to mulch, too?"

"Piper loves to mulch," Michael said, winking. "Back in Pensacola, she was the mulch queen."

Nicole walked up with her mom. "I don't remember mulching in Pensacola."

"You're right, Nicole," I said. "Mulching is a new thing."

Then I heard another familiar voice. "Hey, Snapper!" It was Arizona. She was standing right next to me, grinning like I was her best friend. And for some reason, I was glad to see her.

"This is Arizona," I told them. "This is Michael and Nicole. We're old friends from Pensacola.

Douglas cleared his throat.

"Oh, sorry. And this is Douglas, Michael's friend."

"Hi," Arizona said, staring down at Michael's T-shirt. "Do you skateboard?"

"Yep," Michael and Douglas said together. Then they hollered, "It's the life!" and gave each other high fives.

I couldn't help it. I felt like I was turning green with jealousy. But then I quickly forgot about it because it was time to work. We filled the wheelbarrows with mulch and took turns rolling them over to the beds, where our parents spread it around the plants.

The first time I took my turn with the wheelbarrow, I accidentally tripped and went

headfirst over it, landing sprawled-out on the other side. A hand reached to help me up, and it belonged to Douglas.

"Thanks," I said, a bit embarrassed.

"Wow, Piper," he said. "That was amazing. You really ought to try skateboarding." He didn't say it like Tori would have, in a sarcastic way. He said it like he meant it. Then he quickly added, "But you might want to wear a helmet."

That's how the day went—the wind crisp and cool, mixed in with a lot of fun. And it didn't end there.

Before we left, Mom asked, "Would you like to join us for pizza, Arizona? The Austins and Douglas are going, too."

"Wow! Thanks," she said. "Let me go ask my mom." She dashed across the parking lot, where Mrs. Welch and her husband were loading their shovels into the trunk of the car.

That night, we sat around the table eating pizza at Harry's Pizza Parlor. I told Arizona, "I might like to try that stamp collecting thing for real."

"That would be razzle-dazzle, Snapper!"

I frowned. "Why do you call always call me Snapper?"

Arizona grinned so big I could see the cheese threaded between the gaps in her teeth. "I give all my best friends nicknames."

When she said that, I didn't mind being called Snapper at all. It kind of felt special, like a secret between two friends.

Douglas began to do a million straw paper tricks. We all cracked up. It reminded me of old times in our club. For a moment, I closed my eyes and visualized a new Gypsy Club. I saw Arizona there and Douglas, too. I opened my eyes, and without thinking, I asked, "Hey, Douglas, do you want to be a Gypsy?"

Douglas turned the straw paper into a mustache and said in a deep voice, "Sure, little lady."

"I was wondering when we were going to have a meeting," Nicole said.

"Yeah," Michael chimed in. "It's about time."

"Sounds like fun," said Douglas.

"Don't forget about me," Arizona said.

"But I didn't think you wanted to be in my club," I said.

Arizona shook her head. "I never said that. I said I'd think about it. And I've thought about it. The Gypsy Club sounds razzle-dazzle."

Then Douglas pulled off a slice of pepperoni and flicked it across the table. He was aiming at Michael, but it flew all the way over and hit Mr. Austin in the cheek.

Mr. Austin frowned. "Hey, who did that?"

Chief turned around and looked at me suspiciously.

"Sorry," Douglas said.

"That's okay," Mr. Austin said, and flicked the slice back Douglas's way.

Douglas held the slice over his head with

his fingers. "Introducing the world's smallest Frisbee."

We all laughed, but decided to keep our pepperoni on the pizza where it belonged. I could see why Michael liked Douglas. Maybe he could teach me how to skateboard.

When I got home that night, I added one more thing to my try-new-things list.

5. *Make friends with Arizona and Douglas.*

And then I crossed it off.

14

~~~

GET OFF THE BUS, PIPER, REED!

When next Saturday arrived, I went downstairs to make chocolate chip cookies. It was an unusually warm winter day, and Sam's club was meeting outside. They were planning a pet show. I wonder where she got that idea. Even if she had copied me, it was working. All twelve kids showed up for the planning.

When Mom came downstairs and smelled

the cookies baking, she asked, "Mind if I have one?"

"Go for it, Mom."

Before taking a bite, she said, "The Reed household is going to be Club Central today."

Then the doorbell rang. I wiped my hands and went to open the door. Waiting on the other side were Michael, Nicole, Douglas, and Arizona. Douglas and Michael wore their skateboard T-shirts. This time it didn't bother me. Maybe I'd get one, too. Maybe I'd make it a rule that everyone in our club had to wear them to the meetings.

"Come on in," I said, motioning them to the kitchen table.

Everyone sat except for me. I went over to the kitchen counter and picked up the cookie platter and placed it in the middle of the table.

"Welcome to the first official Norfolk Gypsy

Club meeting," I said. "Who wants a chocolate
chip cookie?"

"I do," said everyone except Nicole.

"I—" Nicole started to say, but I interrupted
her.

"I know, Nicole. You're allergic to chocolate.

That's why I saved you one of Sam's Goldfish Club orange cupcakes." I pulled one off Sam's tray and gave it to her. Then I sat between her and Arizona.

Nicole took a tiny bite. "Yummy," she said, flashing her new smile. Orange streaked each tooth. Sam always used too much food color.

I laughed. Then Michael, Douglas, and Arizona saw what I was laughing at, and they started to crack up, too.

Nicole looked down at her shirt as if she was checking for crumbs. "What?" she asked. "What's so funny?"

"Nicole, your teeth must miss wearing those colored rubber bands," I said.

She tilted her head to the right and scrunched up her nose. "Huh?"

"Look in the mirror, sis," said Michael.

I pointed to the downstairs bathroom, and

Nicole hurried to see what we were laughing at. Soon we heard, "Oh, no!"

After she returned, Nicole ate the bottom part of her cupcake and left the top with the orange frosting.

"Is everyone ready to recite the Gypsy Club Creed?" I asked.

"I don't know it," Douglas said.

"Me neither," said Arizona. "We'll listen today and learn it for the next meeting."

"Sure," I said, handing them each the creed I'd written the night before. Tori had even checked it for me to make sure I'd spelled all the words correctly. "This should help." I understood.

Since moving to Norfolk, I had become an expert at learning new things. When I looked around the table at my friends—old and new—I realized *all* Navy brats were experts at learning new things.

After the meeting, I wrote an e-mail to
Stanley.

Dear Stanley,
I made a list for me, but you're special,
and I think this one might help you, too.

What I've Learned So Far in Norfolk

1. *Whether you move or stay in one place, you have to be open to new things.*

2. *If you're not good at one thing, you'll find something that you are good at. I'm not a great bowler, but I'm pretty good at:*

    a. *swapping stamps,*

    b. *making chocolate chip cookies,*

    c. *mulching,*

    d. *making new friends.*

3. *Sometimes you just have to visualize and believe. When I finally visualized a new Gypsy Club and believed that it could happen, I had a new Gypsy Club.*

I can't wait to see you at spring break. When you get here, I'll teach you to skateboard. That's one more thing I plan to be pretty good at. I'm already visualizing it!

Your pal,

Piper

P.S. Norfolk is a get-off-the-bus place with Arizona smack in the middle of it!